For Charles Kane Huget (he knows why)
—J.L.H.

For Rosalie—and for Deborah and Nat,
who made a room for her
—E.K.

Text copyright © 2010 by Jennifer LaRue Huget
Illustrations copyright © 2010 by Edward Koren

All rights reserved. Published in the United States by Schwartz & Wade Books,
an imprint of Random House Children's Books, a division of Random House, Inc., New York.

Schwartz & Wade Books and the colophon are trademarks of Random House, Inc.

Visit us on the Web! www.randomhouse.com/kids

Educators and librarians, for a variety of teaching tools, visit us at www.randomhouse.com/teachers

Library of Congress Cataloging-in-Publication Data
Huget, Jennifer LaRue.
How to clean your room in 10 easy steps / Jennifer LaRue Huget ; illustrated by Edward Koren.—1st ed.
p. cm.
Summary: A young girl provides unique advice on how to tidy a bedroom.
ISBN 978-0-375-84410-2 (trade)—ISBN 978-0-375-96410-7 (glb)
[1. Housekeeping—Fiction. 2. Humorous stories.] I. Koren, Edward, ill. II. Title.
PZ7.H872958How 2009
[E]—dc22
2008048824

The text of this book is set in Bulmer.
The illustrations are rendered in pen-and-ink and watercolor on paper.
Book design by Rachael Cole

MANUFACTURED IN MALAYSIA
10 9 8 7 6 5 4 3 2 1
First Edition

How To CLEAN YOUR ROOM

in 10 easy steps

by Jennifer LaRue Huget • illustrations by Edward Koren

schwartz & wade books • new york

Welcome to my room. You will notice that it is very clean.

I'm going to show you how you can clean yours, too.

The first thing we need is a messy room. The messier, the better.

There. That's perfect.

Okay, let's get started. Here's how to clean your room in 10 easy steps.

You can pretend you're
too busy to hear.

Or you can answer her. Say, "But
my room isn't messy. I know *exactly*
where everything is!"

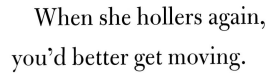

When she hollers again,
you'd better get moving.

Pull everything out of your drawers
and closet and shelves.
Every Single Thing.

All your marbles

and your dolls and their eensy-beensy little shoes

and your bracelets and barrettes

and birthday cards

and that piece of birthday cake and the library books
and your rubber-band ball and your jump rope and
your penny collection.

While you're working, it is okay to talk to yourself.
Try "Oh, I forgot I had this!"

Dump it all in the middle of the room.

Then plunk yourself down, pick a doll out
of the pile, and braid her hair until someone
comes up to scream at you again.

Divide your big pile
into three different piles:

One pile of stuff that's broken.

One pile of stuff you're too grown-up to play with anymore.

And one pile of things that you love more than anything else in the world and want to keep forever and ever.

Put the first two piles into a big box. Stick one of your birthday cards and that piece of cake on top so it will look like a gigantic present.

Drag the box across the hall to your sister's room. Leave it there.

4

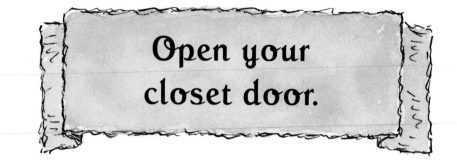
Open your
closet door.

Shove the pile of
things you love inside.
Close the door as
tight as you can.

Watch out. It might explode.

15

Carefully arrange all your stuffed animals on your bed.

This will take a very long time because you've been given lots for every birthday and holiday since you were born. So that's like three gazillion stuffed animals in all.

It's very important that you stop to remember every single animal's name.

Your mother might come in and say, "Sweet Pea, maybe you should think about getting rid of some of those old animals. How about that silly rabbit who's missing one eye and part of an ear?" If this happens, hug that rabbit tight and cry,

"NO! Not Poofball! She's my favorite bunny in the whole wide world!"

When your mother has left the room, toss Poofball back onto the heap and forget about her.

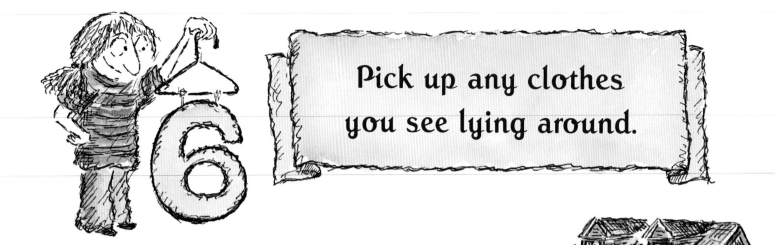

Pick up any clothes you see lying around.

Don't waste time trying to figure out if they're dirty or clean.

Wad them all up into balls and put them somewhere where they won't get in the way. Under the bed is good. Of course, you can always stuff a bunch in the laundry hamper.

Or you could put on
a fashion show!

Put your books back on your shelf.

It's okay if some are upside down or stuck in backward so you can't read the titles. Your bedroom isn't the library, silly!

Or you could pretend it *is* a library and put your books in alphabetical order—going by the main character's name. Cinderella, then the Grinch. Then that kid Jack who climbed the beanstalk . . .

Sit on the floor and read some of your old favorites. If your mother gets mad at you for dawdling, act surprised and say, "But I thought you liked it when I read."

Look carefully for evidence
of snacks you've snuck
into your room.

Candy wrappers
should be gathered up
and saved in your sock
drawer. You will need
them later for crafts, like
making little rugs and
curtains for your doll
house. Or friendship
rings for all your very
best friends. Or pretty
paper flowers to give
to your mom.

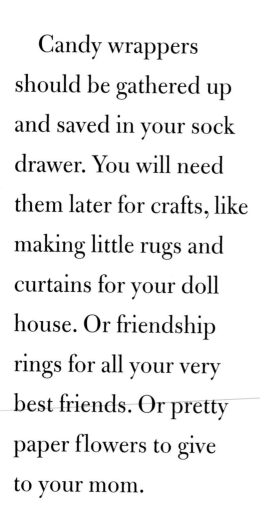

Half-finished cups of milk may be placed in the hamper. (Don't worry: the clothes in there need washing anyway.) Unless the cups are growing mold. Then they are science projects and need to be stored under your bed so you can check on them from time to time.

Pizza crusts may be munched on if they are less than a month old. If you can't remember how old they are, go over to your sister's room and give them to her.

Time to make the bed!

Knock those gazillions of stuffed animals off.

If they look sad and chilly, you can make them nice cozy sleeping bags out of toilet paper.

Now pull the pillow and the blanket and the top sheet off. If you find any dirty socks or undies, stick them under the bed.

Spread the sheet out until it covers the whole bed. If one side hangs over the edge too far, tug on the other side to make it even. Hum while you work so your mom will know you're busy. Keep going back and forth until you get dizzy. Then just give up.

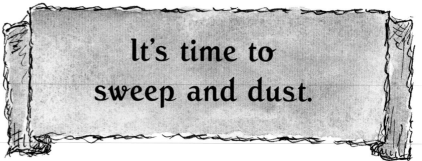

Dusting is easy. Just take a sock from under the bed and skooch it along the edge of your dresser. This is the only place that your mother ever checks. Don't forget to put that sock back where you found it!

Or, as an extra treat for her, skip the sock and use your finger to doodle fancy designs in the dust.

Sweeping is easy, too. Grab a broom and chase the
dust bunnies around with it. When they've settled down
again, scoop up as many as you can with your hands.
Stash them in the sock drawer with the candy wrappers.
You know, for crafts.

(Bonus step!)

Stand in your doorway and admire your beautiful clean room. Give yourself a pat on the back for a job well done.

Okay, now that your room is clean, I'm going to show you how to fix your hair.